THE TICKLISH PALADIN AND THE FOOT PERV

Saber Bhafelheim

Saber Writes

Disclaimer:

All characters are 18 or older. This story is a work of fiction and does not reflect on any persons living or dead. This story contains NSFW erotica, foot fetish, tickle fetish, and more.

This Story was Commissioned by AceBlue27

Prelude

"See, Pidge, I don't know why Keith is always so high and mighty about *everything*"

"Ugh." Pidge sighs, not even bothering to look up at the young paladin. She was buried in her work, and they were piling up enough as it is. As much as she wanted to entertain her friend, she simply had no free time available to sit and play therapist to Lance. "I don't know, why don't you do something about it instead of bitching about Keith to me."

A loud clunk did, however, make her turn her head towards the source of the sound. As soon as she saw Lance's hands hover over a dent gadget, the veins on her forehead popped. She squinted her eyes in silence, watching Lance put the item back where it was.

"Oops! Ha ha!" Lance rubs the back of his head. "So what's all this stuff?"

"Highly experimental tech and *not toys*. D-rings. A portable Stasis Field. Tech Jammers. Noise Dampener. Roly Polies. Badonkadonks. They're not tested for the field yet."

"You know.." A light bulb pops over Lance's head, coming up with the best idea he has ever had. "Why don't I borrow some of these, test them for ya, and come back with the results?"

"If it will get you off my back, fine." Pidge rolled her eyes, tapping her comm unit. A moment later, Lance's unit lit up with a new message. "There. The manuals are in that file. Now don't come back until you've *thoroughly tested them*."

"Oh, don't you worry about that!" Lance smirks, coming up with a million ideas on how to prank Keith with them. "I'll make sure the tests are *thorough*."

The night was young, but Keith was completely exhausted. It was a long day of training, and it didn't help that the hot-blooded Lance kept digging at him the whole time. Being the leader of his squad was stressful enough without Lance being extra thorny in his side today; and he's just had enough. All he wanted to do was take a shower, wash away the day's grime, and pass out in bed. His muscles ached from being so tense all the time, and to be honest, most of that was Lance's fault. At least he had the day off tomorrow, and he wouldn't be stuck married to the idiot the whole time.

Keith threw the towel around his neck to the floor in his otherwise obsessively neat room, and flopped down on the bed. He really should have put some pants on, but he barely had the energy to keep his eyes open. The station had climate control and he was wearing his red shorts, so whatever, it wasn't like he'd freeze. It took all of half a second for Keith to pass out, sleeping soundly, unaware of the soon-to-be intruder outside his door.

Lance waited patiently, on the other side of the door. Earlier in the day, he had already broken into Keith's room once, putting down a spy camera on his desk to find out when Keith would be completely out. As Lance suspected, Keith didn't notice a thing out of place. The copper-skinned paladin stuck one of the technological knick-knacks he got from Pidge on the door, directly over its electronic lock, and tapped his wristwatch, activating the lock-jammer and opening Keith's door as he did before.

Lance snorted upon entering when he heard Keith's light snoring; closing the door behind him. With the way he conducted himself, Lance never expected Keith to be one to display such a sight when he was out like a light. Lance approached Keith's bed, tiptoeing as much as he could. Not that he needed to, though. Keith was completely unconscious, and at that point anything short of a supernova imploding on itself wouldn't have stirred him from his deep slumber.

Lance held the portable Stasis Field out, plotting out the best way to freeze Keith on his bed for his whole day off tomorrow. It would be hilarious. The noise dampener he got from Pidge could be used to muffle and silence the whole room, and nobody would be the wiser. Everyone would have assumed Keith was out doing his own thing, and Keith would be stuck there until Lance comes to the rescue.

The copper-toned paladin took a second look at the device in his hand, and then noticed something else in the corner of his eye. Keith was sleeping topless, with no blankets covering either his torso, groin, or his legs. Lance followed the curvatures of Keith's lower body until he reached Keith's feet, and gasped. It wasn't the first time he had seen Keith barefooted, but he couldn't just stare at those pasty white feet at his leisure then, unlike his situation now. His eyes were fixated on the sleeping paladin's feet, tracing its shape and curves from the ankles to the toes, then from the toes down the arches.

Practically perfection.

Distracted by Keith's feet, Lance's bulge pulsed, tickling him and alerting him to another desire he wanted to act upon. Rethinking his prank, Lance decided that maybe he could do better. Maybe there was another way to teach Keith a lesson, but to also satisfy his inner yearnings. Something a little different. But what?

He supposes he *could* freeze Keith in place now, and have his way with those feet. But that's too easy. Plus, these were experimental tech. There's no way that he could guarantee it won't break down halfway through, and the last thing he wants is to have a pissed off Keith on his ass, giving him a taste of his own medicine. Lance knew that in a fair fight, Keith would have the upper hand, as he always did. No, he needed a different strategy for this.

Lance rummaged through his bag, looking for something else to use, and picked up on the D-rings that Pidge had allowed him to borrow. He recalled reading the manuals about them, how they're meant to temporarily detach a limb; in the rare event that a pilot had their hand or foot caught in a wreckage and couldn't be removed or safely operated on, the D-rings could act as a life-saving device while only sacrificing the limb affected. The applications were limited, however, since they served no real offensive military purpose.

That didn't stop Lance from giving them a different purpose as he had decided what to do to Keith. Working as quickly as he could, Lance snapped the D-rings around Keith's ankle, then immediately activated them. Keith's ankles popped off just as he expected, still attached through the portal, but otherwise completely modulated and separated from his limbs. Lance took the severed feet from the sleeping Keith, and quickly placed them in his bag, smirking as he sneakily stole Keith's feet in his sleep. That should be plenty to play with, Lance though, and plenty to keep himself busy for *his* relaxing day off tomorrow.

Before he could leave, though, there were just two more things he needed to do. Lance took the sound dampener from his bag, and stuck it underside of Keith's desk. With a tap on his wristwatch, the device activates with a bright flash, scanning the room and forming a barrier against its walls, isolating Keith's room from all the sounds from outside, and all the noises in the barrier that could be heard from the outside. Lance held his breath, surprised by the sudden flash that wasn't in the manual, afraid that it might have woken Keith. To his good fortune, though, Keith stayed passed out, completely unaware of the intruder and all that he had done inside his private sanctuary.

Satisfied with his set up now, Lance placed a spare phone next to Keith's bed side, and stole Keith's phone away. Without knowing the passcode, Keith couldn't operate the phone at all; and Lance could always remote access his own device from anywhere. Chuckling to himself, Lance leaves Keith to his slumber, grinning at the round, smooth stumps that were now at the end of Keith's legs, and made his way out of the room. As he turned, he noticed Keith's worn socks laying on the floor, next to the rest of his discarded clothes. Lance debated for a second, then kicked his shoes and stripped his own well-worn socks, dropping them on the floor, before bending over and picking Keith's socks up; stealing a quick sniff of them, Lance sighed at the smell. Dropping them away in his bag, Lance slipped his feet back into his shoes, and took off with his prizes, eager to enjoy them to a fuller extent later. As soon as he closed the door, the mechanism automatically locked itself with a click. Tapping his wrist watch one more time, the Tech Jammer worked in reverse, and jammed the door shut, locking Keith inside. Without Lance manually unlocking it via his watch, there was no way Keith could get out, short of busting the door open; and Lance doubts that even Keith could take down a fire-proof door bare-handed.

It was early morning when Lance's alarm went off. He reached to slam on the snooze button as he always would, and in his daze wondered why he had set the alarm up so early. He turned away, covering his head with his blanket, ready to sleep in for another hour or two, when he suddenly remembered he had Keith's soles up and ready to go. He had set the alarm a good five minutes before when Keith usually wakes up just for this; and he'd be damned if he didn't take full advantage of it. Lance jumped from where he laid down, tangled from his bedsheets, and rolled off his bed, madly throwing hands to free himself of the mess. Activating a duplicate noise dampener in his room for privacy, Lance turned his TV on and switched it to broadcast the spy cam he had set up in Keith's room. Seeing that Keith was still in bed, Lance breathed a sigh of relief. He didn't want to miss a single moment of this.

Like clockwork, Keith woke up precisely five minutes after Lance's alarm went off. The paladin rubbed the sleepiness from his eyes, and pushed himself up, turned his legs towards the side of the bed, and promptly stumbled to the floor, face first. Lance laughed out loud when he saw the predicament that Keith was in, and the confused look on his face was priceless. Keith's mouth was wide open when he looked down to see his feet missing, but when he wiggled his toes, he could still feel them. They were just not where they should have been.

Lance giggled madly, like a child who had gotten away with having done something naughty, and it was his time to brag about it. He remote accessed the phone in Keith's room, then connected the device with his own, allowing him to converse with his leader.

"Good morning, *sunshine*!" Lance bit his tongue, trying his best to not laugh aloud. Sitting on his bed, he looked over at Keith's upturned soles on the oval, metallic plate that was the portable stasis field, which he had set up only a moment ago. "Did you sleep well?"

"...Lance! Why am I not surprised it's always you?!" Keith gritted his teeth, but now it all makes sense. Who else but Lance would do something as weird and childish as this?

"Whatttt? I'm just trying to get to know you better. If we're going to be a team, we need to know more about each other." Lance chuckled. "I'm just trying to put my foot in the door."

"Grrr!" Keith growled, not at all amused with Lance's pun. "What do you want?!"

"Well, for starters. What's your favorite food? Your favorite color?"

"Screw this!" Keith tried to balance himself, but failed to do anything more than get on his knees. Crawling towards the metallic door, Keith tried to turn the handle, but after a few clicks figured out that Lance must have locked him in, too. The paladin leader banged his fist on the door as hard as he could, trying to get someone to notice time, but failing to realize that absolutely no sound could be heard from the outside, thanks to the sound dampening field. "Anyone? Hello? Is anyone outside? I'm stuck here!!"

"Ha ha! Nobody will hear you. I've soundproofed your room, Keith." Lance chuckled, hovering his hand over Keith's soles. "Come on, get back to the bed. You're not leaving until we're done!"

"Screw that, and screw you!" Keith spat back at Lance's voice, unfazed by his demands.

"Well, if you want to do it the hard way, fine by me!" Lance licked his lips, then pressed a finger against the center of Keith's upturned sole.

"Ahmpff..!" Keith gasps, surprised by the sudden touch.

"What was that?"

"Nothing! Screw you, Lance!"

"Okay then!" Lance silently giggled to himself, knowing he definitely heard a reaction from Keith's side. Slowly, he wagged his finger against Keith's sole, circling around the balls of his foot, then took it down his arches.

"Akhmm! Akff!" Keith tried his best to fight the giggles from escaping from his lips, but he couldn't stop his body from suddenly expelling air from his lungs, forcing the pseudo-laughter from him.

"I'm sure I heard you say something, Keith, can you repeat that?"

"Ah've said n-nothing!" Keith bit his lips harder, as Lance's finger started drawing circles on his heel.

"Why don't we do a trust exercise, like a good team would, Keith?" Lance suggested, giggling much more than Keith was. He loved watching the way Keith struggled on his TV; especially since he was unaware that Lance was seeing his every move. "Go sit on your bed and I'll stop tickling you!"

"No!" Keith instantly snapped, only for Lance to scratch along the side of his foot, which was one of his weak spots. "Aha! No! No!!"

“I have all day, Keith.” Lance touched the side of Keith’s foot again, and saw Keith shudder as he did. “I’ll keep touching this spot right here if you don’t!”

“No…! Pffft! Stop! I’m going to the bed, but it’s not because you wanted me to!” Keith crawled on his knees back towards his bed, and climbed onto it the best he could.

“*Good boy.*” Lance teased.

“Screw you, Lance!”

“Come on, Keith. I have a lot of team building exercises for us to do!” Lance smirked. “I just want us to get to know each other better. It’s for the good of the paladins!”

“Why do I doubt everything you’re saying, Lance?” Keith gritted his teeth, his blood pressure increasing by the second.

“Like, for one. I can’t believe you’re the team leader, but you can’t be bothered to keep your feet clean. Peee-ew!” Lance faux-complains, taking the bottle of water and a rag he had prepared from his night stand. Lance turned the bottle into the rag, soaking it in cold water, and then held it up, grinning the whole time. “Since I’m such an awesome guy, I’ll clean your feet for you just this one time, okay?”

“Don’t you dare touch my feet again!!” Keith shouted, scrambling to take Lance’s phone in his angry, gripping hands.

“Oh hello, there you are!” Lance looked into the video call, and smiled at the angry face Keith was making.

“You bastard! Leave me feet alone, and come get me out of my room!!”

“Like I said, we’ll get there when we get there. *After* our team building exercise.” Lance showed the rag to Keith, and ignored the angry noises Keith made. The copper-skinned paladin began to rub the rag across the severed feet, wiping them down one long, slow stroke at a time. The little nooks of the rag scratched against Keith's feet, making him inhale and exhale sharply whenever they got near one of his more sensitive spots.

"Hmmmmph!!" Keith whined, to Lance's delight. "Stop! Stop! My feet are clean enough!!"

It wasn't entirely untrue. Keith's body wash lingered on Keith's feet, even after a night of rest. Having been aired out by Lance, they didn't smell bad at all; but that didn't stop Lance from pretending they needed to be cleaned and put through the first of many of his devious plans. It wasn't just water in the bottle, but it wasn't like Keith could tell with just a wet rag. He had put a couple drops of a sensitivity potion in there, which would soak through the skin and make Keith's feet more and more ticklish as time went on. Lance vigorously rubbed and scrubbed Keith's soles with the rag, making sure both soles were thoroughly moist by the end, allowing every inch of them to absorb the chemicals for the rest of his hellish day.

"See, Keith. I can, in fact, do something nice for you. Now that your feet are all clean, why don't you do something nice for me, for a change?"

"Screw you, Lance!!" Keith's face was red and puffy with anger. "Never!"

"Well, we know how this goes, don't we?" Lance picked up a stiff feather from his collection of tools, and showed it to Keith on the camera. "We need to trust each other, Keith, and I'm going to give you a chance to trust me."

"No!!"

"Okay, well, it's your funeral!" Lance lowered the feather, and dug between Keith's toes. Spinning the stiff, fuzzy feather tip, between Keith's big and second toe, Keith immediately loses it, despite having done his best to hold everything in so far.

“Eeheehe! Eheehe! No! Stop! Lance!”

“So, how about that trust exercise?”

“Damnit! Fine! Heeheehee! What do you want me to do-ooh-hoo?”

“Easy. I want you to spread your toes for me, Keith. Just spread your toes wide.” Lance smirked.

“Screw that! You’ll just us-ooh-hoo-use it to tickle me more!!” Keith clamps both his hands over his mouth, trying to stop himself from laughing.

“Tsk tsk tsk, Keith. So untrusting, so uncooperative. I’m afraid you’ll have to be punished.” Lance clicked his tongue, but secretly loved the fact that Keith resisted so much. He didn’t want an easy win, anyway; and de-feet-ing Keith like this will make his victory all the sweeter.

Lance tapped on his wristwatch, activating the app for the stasis field that Keith’s feet sat on. It was a thing of bio-engineering marvel, really. Practically a thing of war crime, if anyone else had gotten their hands on it. The manuals made the operations simple enough to understand. It was voice activated, and Lance controlled it by speaking into the mic on his wrist watch. In addition to immobilizing something, however, it seemed that Pidge had added an untested upgrade, which could force simple commands onto any victims of the stasis field.

“Spread the toes, and hold.” Lance spoke into his wrist watch, and sat in anticipation as the device whirl to life. The metallic plate projected a hologram like that of a digital mesh, which covered both of Keith’s soles. After a quick scan, Keith’s toes seemed to have spread themselves to the fullest.

“What the hell was that?!” Keith protested, having felt his feet move on their own. His toes were forcefully spread apart, and now he had lost any and all mobility in them. It felt like they were encased in solid concrete, but there was nothing but air around them.

"*That,* my dear leader, is your punishment!" Lance smiles a wide smile. He immediately returns Keith's soles to the attention of his feather, dipping and sawing them between Keith's now unwillingly fanned toes, making sure the stiffness of it brushes against the sensitive skins between those immobile, frozen digits. As he spun the feather along the side of the toes, Keith began to chuckle harder and harder, unable to contain the laughter from within him anymore.

"Ha ha ha! Ha ha ha ha! You're so-ho ho ho dead!"

"That's not very team-like, Keith!" Lance teases, making his way now to the pinky toe. As soon as the feather touched Keith's pinky toe, the paladin leader's laughter lit up like a christmas tree, and Lance noticed that the reaction was so much more violent than when he had brushed the other toes. Trying to confirm his theory, Lance took the feather and sawed them between the big and second toe once more, noting that Keith's laughter, while still loud, died down from when it was on his pinkie toe. Doing a final check, Lance oved the feather back to the pinkie toe, and immediately knew that this was another of Keith's weak spots, as Keith screeched his head off.

"HA HA HA! HA ha AAAAAH ha ha! DEAD!! HA HA HAAH!! Lance!! LANCE!! HAH AAH! YOU AAAHH HA HA DEAD!!"

"I'm telling you now, Keith. That kind of attitude isn't fit for a leader. You need to calm down, and put more trust in me!"

"HA HA HA!! NOO! NEVA-AH HA-HAHA!"

"Then we continue the trust building exercise!" Lance replied, dropping the phone down on his bed, as does the feather. Keith's laughter only died down for a moment before flaring back up again, when Lance replaced the feather with a cold, metallic fork. Lance licked his lips as he readied the pointy end at the other foot -- the one that was spared from the feather's torture, and raked the prongs up and down Keith's arches, making so to go slow enough that every wrinkle was dug into.

"Ha ha HA HA HA! W-a-aaah is thaaaaa-aaaaaha-aht!" Keith screamed, seeing only the ceiling of Lance's room now.

"Let's play a game. Why don't you try to guess what tool I'm using. I'll keep using it until you get it right!"

"Naaaww!! Nooooaaahahahaha!" Keith shouted, the assault on his feet made it impossible for him to think. The four pronged fork might as well have been a hundred pronged, their sharpness scratched cruelly along his sole, sending ticklish signals from his feet directly into his brain. He wanted to wiggle his toes, to clench them shut, to help with the ticklish sensation; but he couldn't do it, no matter how hard he tried. Whatever Lance had used to keep his soles immobile was stronger than the strength he could muster. "Waahaaahaaa!! Whaaat is that!! Oh god! Oh god! Ohh ho ho hooooo!!"

"Come on, leader! Don't you know what this is?" Lance blew a raspberry between his lips, laughing along with Keith as he continued to rake the fork all over. He held the fork like a pencil, and pretended it was a mini-rake, working his way on a zen garden that is Keith's soles. Lance drew circles along the balls of Keith's foot, spirling it, leaving a ticklish trail on his skin, as though he was taking care of a real zen garden. The lines dissipated as quickly as they were drawn; but that wasn't an issue. He could just go over the immobile soles once more! "I'll give you a hint! It's got four prongs at one end!"

"Fa-haa-haahaa! It's a faaa-aaahh-haaa-haa-haaak!"

"What was that?" Lance laughed, "I can't hear you!"

"It's a FORK! HAAA HAAA HAAAAAA!!!" Keith cried, loudly. "Now STAAA-HAA-HAA-AHPT!"

"Bingo! That's one!" Lance picks out another tool. "Now, what's this?"

"No! Nooh ho ho ho!" Keith screamed, already feeling Lance working the second mystery object between his toes. Something was forced between them, as Lance weaved them over, then under, and over again. When Lance was finished, he began to pull them from side to side, sawing and flossing the most sensitive parts at the base of his toes. "NOOO!!! HAA HAA HAA!! HAA HAA HAA!! STOP!! STAH-AAH-AAAH-AAAPT!"

"We're no strangers to the game, you know the rules and so do I!" Lance teases.

"It scratches!! Ha ha ha! It scratches soo-ohh-ho-ho bad!" Tears began to fill Keith's face as he felt like his toes were on fire. "A string! Ha haha haaaaa!! Dental floss!! Nooo-oohhh ohhhh! Lance stop! Aaah ha! Aaaah ha ha! Scratchy! Scraaaa-aaah-aaah-tchy!!"

"What is it, Keith?" Lance chuckled. "What am I using?"

"A pipe cleeee-eeeeh-eeeeheee-heee-hee-ner!!"

"Correct again, Keith." Lance pulled the pipe cleaner away from Keith's toes, giving one final scratch before they were free of its infernal fuzziness. "And now, can you get three for three?"

Lance paused, delaying the third object for dramatic effect. Keith still giggled, waiting in anticipation and horror of what terrible object Lance has decided to use to wreak havoc on his feet this time.

The seconds passed, and Lance's heart throbbed. He hesitated, wondering what excuse he could use if he were caught. He pushed the phone a little further away, just in case. He didn't want Keith to accidentally catch a glimpse or anything. Taking a deep breath to calm his nerves, though, he smelled the tickle sweat that Keith's soles had produced from his session so far, and his bulge grew harder. He took another sniff of Keith's sweaty, aromatic soles, building up his nerves and desires, and went for it.

Lance leaned in, and took a long, slow lick, with just the tip of his tongues. He traced it all the way from the heels to Keith's toes, careful to not breathe over them, or to touch the soles with his lips. As soon as his tongue reached the end of Keith's big toe, he pushed himself away, only to hear Keith screaming in laughter.

"HA HA HA!! WHAT!! WAAA-AAAAH-AAAHHT IS THATTTT!!"

He could barely register what he had just done. Stealing a taste of Keith's amazing soles was probably the bravest, most foolish thing he had ever done in his life. Keith's flavor lingered in his mouth, as he smacked it a couple of times to get the taste down. He needed another hit. Holding his breath once more, Lance leaned forward to the foot he hadn't yet licked, and traced the tip of his tongue across the fleshy base of the toes, tasting the fresh sweat between the immobile digits. Despite being a shorter distance than the lengthwise of the foot, Lance took more time going slower, and wagged his tongue as he licked across, making sure each section of Keith's under-toe got tasted. Lance almost couldn't hold back a moan as the flavor of Keith's toes penetrated his mind, like a sniper trashing a target from a mile away.

"AHH!! AAAAHHH!! AAAHHHA HA HA HA!! WHAT DA-AH-HA-HAHA-HELL!! A BRUSH?? A DAMNED BRA-HA HA HA HA-RUSH!"

Keith's heart skipped a beat. He had forgotten they were playing a game with how amazing Keith's soles tasted. He wanted to steal a third lick, but it was far too risky. If Keith got a third dose of it, there is no way Keith wouldn't figure out what he had done.

"Ha! Three for three. You the man, Keith!" Lance lied, covering his tracks. "Yes, it was, in fact, a wet paint brush! See, you're getting the idea of this."

"Screw-hoo hoo hoo you!"

"That's no way to talk. Do you want to go again that badly?" Lance licked his lips, tasting Keith's toes on his tongue still. He was distracted. He wanted another taste. He needed it. He needed to find another chance to steal another lick somewhere, without Keith finding out.

"NO!!" Keith screamed, the bottom of his feet still tingled from the tickling. The part that was wetted by 'a paintbrush' felt cooler as air blew over.

"Then we go back to our trust exercise, Keith." Lance slapped the soles with his hand, getting Keith to yelp at the sudden touch. It wasn't unwelcomed, though. Lance slapped away the rest of the tingling on his sole, which made the ticklishness slightly more bearable.

"Screw you, Lance!!" Keith grunted, breathing heavily. "You've had your fun, now let me out of my room! You're in so much trouble!"

"Yeah? What are you going to do about it, Keith?" Lance smirks.

"W-what?!"

"Are you going to run all the way to the commander? Tell him all about how Lance tickled your little feetsies? Hee hee hee. Yeah, you go and do that, Keith!"

"You bastard!"

"Go. Go now. I'll make the call for you, and he can join in the call, and I can show him exactly what I'm doing to your feet. Would you like that, Keith?"

"Go to hell!"

"Yeah, that's what I thought!" Lance laughed. "So if you want to get out of this, you'll have to complete my trust exercise!"

"God damnit! What else do you want from me?!" Keith growled, angry and frustrated that he's stuck in this situation.

"I'm going to set your feet free from stasis, and you're going to wiggle your toes for me." Lance thought about it, then added. "And if you stop at any time, you lose."

"You creep! And if I win?"

"I will call the whole thing off, and you can enjoy the rest of your day off without me."

"..." Keith was silent for a moment. "Deal."

"Disable stasis." Lance spoke into his wrist watch. "Your five minutes starts now, Keith. Start wiggling."

Keith's face turned red as he began to wiggle and fan his toes. Not because he was being obedient, but because this was his chance at getting out. No matter what Lance says, the moment he's free, he's going to ram Lance down like a tank, and knock that little mother fucker all the way to next Thursday, and then some.

Despite all that, his toes continued to wiggle and wag, just like a good puppy's tail. Lance let out a moan as he watched, with his face next to the wiggling toes, and sighed happily at the show. Keith's tickle abused, sweaty toes gave off the most fragrant aroma, and it made his mouth water. The way they wiggled was so submissive, despite how angry Keith was. The toes fanned and spread to his command, and it was nothing like anything Lance ever witnessed. It was so much better than anything he could come up with in his imagination; and it was then he was glad that he was recording the whole thing. Lance made a mental note to come revisit these toes wiggling at a later time.

The copper-toned paladin allowed Keith to continue his toe-dance for two minutes, making sure that it was a good length of video for his personal use later, before carrying out his sabotage. He had taken a different device from Pidge earlier -- one that he had seen her use, but had no idea what it was for. It looked like a pen, and when activated, the tip of it spun as fast as one would expect a hand drill to. The only difference was, at the end of the needle-thin drill bit sat a metallic sphere instead of the sharpened, corkscrew tip. The ball was no bigger than a grain of rice, but Lance had tried it out on his hand earlier, and felt the tingles it gave off. It would be the personal tool to use against Keith.

Lance clicked on the tool like a pen, and the sphere began to spin and vibrate. The whirring sound was odd to Keith, and it took him a second to register what was happening.

"Lance! No! You said--"

"I said all you have to do is wiggle your toes, Keith. I never said anything else. Now keep wiggling!"

Keith had no choice but to continue wiggling his toes for Lance's sick game, and a second later, felt a strange sensation at the center of his arches. It was a tingle, but the longer it lingered, the odder it felt. It didn't do much when it merely touched him, but when Lance pushed it up against his ticklish, tender, soft flesh, the vibrations rippled out, and Keith howled as the miniature shockwaves assaulted his nerves, penetrating his skin, giving him an incredible itching sensation deep in his flesh. The ticklishness radiated outwards, and felt like his sole was being scratched by tiny hands across a large patch at the same time. Keith cried in anguish, trying his best to keep his toes moving, but the more he wiggled them, the more he pushed his foot against the diabolical tool, and the stronger the vibrations seemed to become.

"HA HA HA HA! What the H-hell! Eee hee hee heeeeheeeeheeeeeeee!"

If his foot was still attached at the ankles, at least he could try and pivot himself away from the attack; but regardless of how he twisted his ankles, Keith's feet stayed on the metallic plate on Lance's bed, unable to budge in any direction.

Lance was having an absolute blast. He had pushed his pillow away to replace it with the metal plate, resting in a comfortable position laying on his stomach. That allowed him to point Keith's toes towards him as they wiggled, and gave him the best view when he pushed the tool into Keith's foot flesh. The buzzing and whirring against his captive souls were music to his ears, much like the inane laughter that came from the video call. He had it set just to the side, so he could keep an eye on Keith's face, while smelling the delicious scent of Keith's toes just off screen.

With Keith's soles tickled to a nice shade of pink, Lance took the vibrating, spinning tool to Keith's toes. He didn't forget about how sensitive his pinkie toe was, and poked the tool directly on it. Keith instantly reacted by clenching his toes close, but that only served to worsen the tickling as the vibrations traveled through his flesh; and made him squeal and moan all the more. Lance tried prodding the base of Keith's pinkie toe, and that's when Keith's foot instinctively tried to grab at the offending thing, gripping it tightly to stop its movements.

"Ha ha HA HA ha ha HA! Not my To-oho ho ho! Nawt my tooo-ho hoho-oh-es!!!"

Lance glanced at his watch, and only four and a minutes have passed, winning him the little wager he had.

"Ha, you lose, Keith!" Lance gloated.

"No-hohoho fair!!"

"Ha! A win is a win. All is fair is love and war!" Lance giggles, letting go of the tool and scratching Keith's sole with his fingers.

"Ha ha ha!! Stop!! Staaaoph!!" Keith yelled, resentful that Lance cheated for a win. "Ha ha ha!! Stop tickling me!! Stop tickling me-eehe hehe heeee!!"

"Ha ha! Imagine, the high and mighty Keith, leader of our little band of paladins, begging for his feet to stop being tickled!" Lance said in a sing-song voice, delighted at the thought.

"Screw you, Lance!" Keith wiped the tickle-tears from his face, already feeling humiliated by what Lance had done.

"Wow, I wouldn't talk like that if I were you." Lance scratched the back of his head. "You know, I was going to offer you a little break from tickling, but clearly you still have plenty of energy left, and I still want to take you down a peg!"

"What!? No!" Lance jumped at it. "I want a break! I want a break!"

"Ha! Are you sure? You're going to have to do me another little favor if you want that break."

"NO TICKLING!!" Keith screamed at the phone, startling Lance a little. "Whatever sick game you want to play, NO TICKLING this time!!"

"Spoil sport." Lance muttered. Sitting back up on the edge of his bed, and taking the phone to see a wrecked Keith, whose face was red and wet with sweat and tears. "If you want to take a break from the tickling, then you have no choice but to play with me."

"Ugh! Fine!" Keith groaned, wiping his face on his discarded shirt. He knew he looked terrible. "What do you want?!"

"I want you to play the little piggies game with me." Lance swapped the video to the front cameras, showing Keith his own severed feet, which looked just as red as he was. "It's simple. I'll do the motions, and I want you to sing the song with me. *Like a team.*"

"Aw, hell. What is wrong with you, Lance?!" Keith complained, but quickly clammed up when he saw Lance's clawed hands hovering in the video, directly over his feet. "Okay! Okay!! Damn it, I'll play! NO TICKLING!"

"I'm just trying to make us more in sync, that's all. Ready?" Lance grabbed one of Keith's big toe with his thumb and index finger, wiggling it as he began to recite the rhyme. "This little piggy went to the market..."

"..The mark-k-ket.." Keith said, being forced to play along, his cheeks burning with embarrassment. He was getting more and more anxious, dreading when Lance would get to his pinkie toe. "This little piggy s-pffft-stayed home."

“This little piggy had roast beef..” Lance moved on to the third toe, then the fourth. “And this little piggy… Keith?”

“Pffft!” Keith tried to hold it in, but the moment Lance touched the fourth toe, he couldn’t help but laugh.

“What happened to the fourth little piggy, Keith?” Lance taunted.

“That little piggy had none!” Keith held in his laughter long enough to reply.

“Well then, and this little piggy..” Lance took Keith’s pinkie toe in his fingers, and squeezed it several times, forcing Keith to burst out in laughter. “Went… Keith, where did this little piggy go?”

“Eeeheehe! No tickling!!! Noo! Noo!”

“I’m going to give you one more chance to not mess up, Keith, or I will tickle these beautiful soles, nonstop, until midnight, and then some!” Lance said, accidentally letting what was in his mind slip.

“Hee hee hee!! What?? What’d you say??”

“I said, do this game right, or I will tickle you non-stop for the rest of the day and all of tonight!” Lance quickly recovered, hoping to god that Keith didn’t hear what he said.

“NO!! I’ll do it right!!” Keith panicked.

“As I was saying. Where did this little piggy go, Keith?” Lance wiggled Keith’s pinkie toe again.

“Hee hee hee!! This little piggy-ee-hee-hee went wee-hee-hee all the way home!!” Keith screamed, knowing that Lance would be tickling all the way down his arches towards his heel; and Lance did exactly that. “Ha ha haaaa!! Ha ha ha! Nooo!!”

“Since you messed up, we’re going to go again, Keith!” Lance said, matter-of-factly. He moved to the other foot, starting at the pinkie toe this time. “This little piggy went to the market..”

"Hee hee hee!! This little piggy stayed ho-oh-oh-oh-ome!!" Keith tried, but failed to contain his laughter. "This little piggy had ro-ho-ho-ho-ast beef! Ha ha ha!! This little piggy had none!! And this little piggy-ee-hi-hi-hiiiii w-went wee-hee-wee-hee-hee-hee heeee! All the way home!!"

"Pathetic! Again! And we're not going to stop until you get it right!" Lance grabbed both of Keith's big toes at the same time. "Last chance, Keith. Get this wrong and I will tickle you until the only thing you will ever dream about are these little piggies!!"

"No ho ho!!" Keith begged, but the game had already started when he felt Lance wiggling both his big toes at thes same time. "This little piggy went to the ma-ha ha ha-ket! This little piggy stayed ho-ho-ho-home! This li-hee-hee-tle piggy-heehee had roast-feet--NO!! ROAST BEEF! ROAST BEEF!!"

"Tsk tsk tsk. What a shame, Keith." Lance burst out in laughter, too. This was going way too good; so much better than he had planned. More importantly, the way Keith said 'roast feet' had just given Lance another brilliant idea. He was a little surprised at himself that he didn't think about it until now; and he had found the finale that he wanted to end the day with. But first, he wanted to play one last game with Keith. "I guess you really want to spend more time with me!"

"No ho ho ho!!! Stop! That was an accident!!" Keith covered his face with a pillow, trying to hide from Lance.

"Nuh uh uh. Put your face back on the video. We're not done yet, Keith."

"Oh, damnit! How much more do you want to put me through?? Haven't I suffered enough already??" Keith shouted, getting mad.

"We can either play a game, or we can go straight to merciless tickling. Which one do you want?"

"You bastard!"

“I’m giving you five seconds to choose. Four. Three. Two--”

“Fine! We’ll play your stupid game!!”

“Ha! I knew you’d see it *our* way.” Lance quickly swiped the bag of tools from his night stand. “This game is very easy. All you have to do is answer all of my questions for you.”

“It can’t be that easy!”

“It’s team building exercises. I just want to get to know you!” Lance said, acting hurt. “Well, okay, if you want to make it more difficult. Here’s a new rule. If you give me an answer that I don’t believe is true, I’m going to start tickling the truth out of you, and I’m not going to stop.”

“No!” Keith spits out immediately. “That is so unfair!”

“You have 15 seconds to answer each question. If you refuse to answer, I tickle you. If you give me a bad answer, I tickle you. If you lie, oh yes, you had better believe I will tickle these little piggies!”

“I don’t want to play this game anymore!” Keith protests.

“Well, if you don’t want to play, we can go back to straight up tickling you until your mind melts into butter! I mean, all you have to do is tell me the truth, and nobody gets hurt, or tickled!” Lance giggles. “I’m okay with that either way.”

“God damnit!” Keith groans. “You absolutely suck, you know that? Fine, what’s your first stupid question?”

“Aw yeah! Let’s go!” Lance smiled to himself, with Keith biting the bait. “First, what’s your favorite color?”

“Easy, red!”

“What, not blue?”

“No! Blue’s a terrible color, worn by terrible people!” Keith claps back.

"Huh. I don't think I like that answer, Keith." Lance picked up a Q-tip, showing it to his friend on screen. "I don't think I like that answer at all!"

"NO! Stop! Okay, fine, blue! I like blue. I love blue! In fact, I *adore* blue!!" Keith had never had to backpedal so fast in his life, especially when it was just to satisfy Lance's sick urges to be the one who's right.

"Ha, that's better." Lance snorted, loving the fact that he could make Keith change what he said so easily. "Second question. What's your favorite food?"

"God, I don't know. Hamburgers?"

"Huh, I'd have pegged you for more of a hot dog kind of guy." Lance said cooly, picking up some dental floss and showing it on screen.

"WAIT! Wait! Well now that I think about it, hot dogs are fantastic, aren't they?"

"Pfft! Ha ha ha!" Lance laughed. "Yeah, they sure are. Now, let's see. Where are you more ticklish, your left foot, or your right foot?"

"Hey! Come on, Lance! That's not fair!"

"Tick tock, Keith. Tick tock." Lance picked up a pen and uncapped it, holding it as though he was ready to write something on Keith's soles.

"My--" Keith's face absolutely smoldered. He could almost feel steam coming off of his cheeks with how warm it was. "Damnit! Lance!!"

"Five, four, three, two--"

"MY LEFT FOOT!"

"Ha ha, well done, Keith. So glad to see you're opening up with me, finally." Lance put the pen down, drunk in the moment. "Next question. Of all the tickling today, which one was your favorite?"

“What the hell! None of them!” Keith immediately snapped back. “Not a single one!”

“That’s not what I want to hear, Keith.” Lance’s hand moved over to the tooth brush, picking it up. “Come on, pick one. Which one was your favorite?”

“No! I’m not going to say I liked any of them because I didn’t!” Keith shouted, angrily. “None! None! None! I didn’t like any of it!”

“Four, three, two..”

“You can’t! You can’t make me say it!”

“Oh, that’s too bad, Keith. Such a shame.” Lance put the brush onto Keith’s toes, and began to slowly draw circles.

“Hee hee! No! Hee hee hee that’s so un-fa-aaii-airr!” Keith was angry, but another wave of giggles were forced out of his mouth, his lips twisted in a wicked grin. “Stop! No ho ho ho! Wait wait! Stop! Ha ha ha ha ha!!”

“Let’s see if you do better with question number five, Keith. Which foot would you prefer I focus on tickling for the rest of this game? Left or right?”

“Ha ha ha! No! Neither! Ha ha ha! Stop tickling m-me-ee-eee-hehe”

The brush scrubbed cruelly over all of Keith’s toes, despite all his cries and pleas. Lance paid special attention to the pinkie toes when it was their turn, and Keith just about lost it with the teasing scrubs. He was laughing so hard that he wasn’t able to answer the next three questions, to which delighted Lance, but because now he got to add another brush to the mix, molesting both of Keith’s pinkie toes at the same time with two stiff brushes that just would not leave the poor digit alone.

“HA HA HA HA! Stop! STaaa-aaa-aaah-hhhaahaa-aph! Hee hee hee heee heeee!!!”

"Heh, how cute is that toe?" Lance whispered to himself.

"Wha-aa-aahht?!"

"What? Nothing?" Lance pressed the brush on the pinkie toe and scrubbed twice as hard, turning Keith's laughter into a maddening scream. He didn't intend for Keith to hear his comment, but he had better tickle that memory out of Keith now!

"HA HA HAAAAAA AAAAAAAAA AAAAAA AAAAAA AAH!!" Keith's voice was starting to become coarse, his head shaking from side to side. The red paladin had long since dropped the phone on the bed as he turned and tossed all over it, trying to get away from the tickling, but having no choice in the matter. "FAA-AAA-AAA-HHAA HAA HAA HAAK YOU, LANCE, HAAA HAAA HA HAAA HAAAAA!!"

"Oh, oh dear!"

"HAAA HAAha HAAA!!"

"Well, that certainly wasn't very team-buildy, now, was it, Keith?"

"FAAA AAAHA HAA HAAA!! AAK YOU, LANNCEEEEEEE!!"

"Well, that settles it, Keith." Lance dropped both of the tooth brushes in his hands, stopping the tickling on Keith's soles. It was time for the grand finale. "Since nothing I've done seemed to have improved your teamwork skills, you have left me no choice!"

"HAAA HAA HA HAAAAA!! Ha ha ha!! Haha hahaha! Stop! Stop! Enough! I've had enough!!" Keith cried, at the edge of his ropes. "This isn't funny anymore, Lance!! Let me out, let my feet go! Fix all of this!"

"Oh, I'll fix you, alright, *twinkle toes*!!" Lance tapped on his wrist watch to activate the stasis field once more. "Spread your toes wide, Lance, and then hold still"

"Lance? Lance? Stop! Stop! Can't we talk about this?" Keith

dreaded the feeling of his feet being taken over once again, with immobility forced upon him. He was genuinely terrified of what Lance had plotted for him, from the way he sounded. He knew that it would be way worse than anything else Lance had done so far. “Come on, Lance, let me off the hook already!”

Lance went to his closet, and took two things back with him One was a bottle, and the other was the heater that he kept on at night sometimes, when it was too cold for his liking. Roast feet. The idea was genius. He was so glad Keith gave it to him, because he would otherwise never have come up with it himself.

“See, Keith, I’m not going to tickle you anymore if you hate it so much.”

“Then what are you doing?!” Keith whined. “Why are you spreading my toes again??”

“I’m not going to tickle you at all, Keith. Hee hee hee!” Lance grabbed the biggest, broadest brush he could find in his tool sack, and opened the bottle, squeezing a clear gel out of it onto both of Keith’s soles.

The cool liquid made Keith gasp, and then giggle again as Lance applied a thick layer of it, brushing it all over both of Keith’s soles. The liquid was thick and heavy; viscous like honey. Lance made sure every part of those soles were covered before leaving them alone. To Keith’s surprise, it didn’t take long before his feet were let off easily, or so he might have thought.

“No, I’m not going to tickle your feet, Keith; but remember what the piggies had from earlier?”

“Roast.. Beef?” Keith answered, dense as he could be sometimes.

“No, that’s not what *you* said!” Lance laughed, as he heard Keith realized what was about to happen.

“Roast.. Oh no! NO! NO NO NO! LANCE! Lance! Stop this at once!”

"Oh yes yes yes! Since you wouldn't play my games, you'll just have to be punished!" Lance laughed the whole time Keith cried out in protest, and set up the heater on his night stand. Plugging it in and turning the temperature dial, Lance made sure it was a safe distance away, but close enough that it wouldn't miss any part of Keith's soles as they got slow roasted. "See, you really should have just played my games!"

"I'll play! I'll play!" Keith screamed, as he felt his soles become warmer and warmer. It wasn't an uncomfortable heat, but the gel began to bubble, and his soles began to tingle. "Wait, what's that? Turn it off! Turn it off, Lance!"

"Ha ha, sorry, can't hear you, Keith! Gotta roast your feet for your hungry little piggies! Ha ha ha!" Lance mocked, picking up his phone again to show Keith a live stream of his increasingly reddening soles.

"Ehe? Ehe?!? What is that? Lance!! What is that?! What did you put on my feet? Eehehe?!" Keith was shocked. Not only were his feet getting warmer, they tingling intensified. The bubbling gel

"Oh, just a special little brew I cooked up! You see, it does absolutely nothing in its gel form.."

"Hee hee hee!! What is thaa-ah-aht!" The tingling had grown on his soles, and they began to itch. First it was his arches, then the balls of his foot, then between his toes, and all around the digits, until every part covered by the gel began to itch, and itch, and itch. "Ha ha ha! HaAA HAAHAA! Lance! It itches! Ha ha ha!! It itches so bad!! Ha ha hahahaaa!!"

"Yeah, the chemical compound somehow changes when it's exposed to heat, and turns into a powder form; and that's still fine, but once you add moisture back into it, it's the absolute worst itching powder you've ever seen!"

Keith could have sworn that he was in literal hell. He had never felt such itching on his feet. He wanted to scratch them, but his feet were held inside the stasis prison, unable to move even an inch; and unlike normal itching powder where it simply won't stick to some parts of the body, the gel helped cover every wrinkle and crease on his soles, making absolutely certain that no parts of his soles were spared the treatment -- especially the small folds on his soles and arches.

"See, the thing with the heat lamp is that when your sweat dries, it doesn't disable the powder, so when you sweat again and make them wet again, the itching powder reactivates! Isn't it genius?!"

"Ha ha ha ha!! HAAHAHAA! Hee hee heeeeeeeheee!" Keith's voice was giving out, but he couldn't stop. He was going insane. "Lance! Laaan-ceee-ahahaha!"

It took no time at all for Keith's walls to come crumbling down, and the poor paladin was rendered giggling, laughing like a madman, begging for Lance to put him out of his misery. "Ahaha! HAHAHAHAHA! Anything!! Ha ha ha! I'll do anything!! HAHAHA! Please just scratch my feet! HAHA! Plee-ee-eeheehee-ese! Scratch!! HAHAHA! It itches so much!! HAHAHA!"

"Well, since you don't want to play games with me, I'll just leave you to entertain yourself!" Lance pretends to get up from the bed, and walks towards his door. "I'll come back in a bit and check on you, but now it's time for food!"

"LANCE!! HA HA HAHAHA!! WAIT!! HAHA, COME BA-AHA-HA-ACK!"

The soles of his feet grew warmer by the second, until it felt like he was standing on hot concrete on the midday of summer. It didn't burn, but it was hot; and he couldn't help but sweat, drenching the itching powder and reactivating each particle that wrecked the nerves on his feet. The itching was everywhere, all at once. There wasn't a single thing Keith could do to escape it. Keith screamed, cried, and begged, wishing for it to end, but knowing that Lance had dropped the call, Keith could only moan and writhe in ticklish agony. The cycle repeated itself as Keith's foot sweat dried, allowing the heat to build up, and another layer of sweat formed, reactivating the powder again and again.

Lance of course was still in his room. He made sure to take photos of Keith's immobile soles that were now being cruelly roasted in its ticklish, hellish cycle. As he snapped, Keith's soles gave off a sweaty scent that mixed with the itching powder, which smelled like sweet cinnamon, and Lance's bugle twitched in his pants as he inhaled the delicious aroma of those poor soles being tormented.

Lance's mouth watered, and he moaned, bringing his nose closer to get a better whiff of those sweet, sweaty toes. They laid still, taking in all the punishment that the heat lamp gave off. Lance wished for nothing more than a chance to taste them again, just like he had stolen a lick earlier. What he wouldn't give for another chance like that, to taste and savor Keith's soles.

What he wouldn't give, indeed.

He pressed a button to connect the call again, and was immediately greeted by the sound of Keith laughing his head off.

"Hey, having fun without me, Keith?"

"HA HA HA!! FA-AHA-HAHAHAK YOU!! FA-AHAHA-K YOU!!!! IT ITCHES!! IT ITCHES HA HA HA!"

"Alright, Keith, I've decided to take you on that deal, after all."

"HAHAAAA!! FUCK YOU!! AAAHAHAHA!!"

"Well, you did say you'd do *anything.* I *could* just come back in an hour and check in on you if you prefer."

"NOHOHOHO!! I'M SOWEE-HEE-HEEHEE!! I'M SOWEE!!"

"That's a better attitude already. See, if you're like this all the time, we wouldn't have so many issues together!" Lance jabs, much to Keith's ticklish annoyance. "I'll scratch your feet and make the tickles go away, IF and ONLY IF you say "Lance is the absolute best, and I'm just a ticklish little paladin!' and say it like you mean it!"

"WHYYY!! AHAHAHA!"

"I'll give you five seconds to decide before I leave and come back in an hour. Five--"

"NO!! NO HO HO! I'LL SAY IT!!" Keith screamed. He couldn't take another hour of this hellhole. "AHA! AHA! LANCE IS THE-BWAHAHA! BEST! THE ABSO-OHOHOHO-LUTE BEST! AN-DHAAHAHA- I'M J-JUST A TICKLISH LI-EE-HEEHEETTLE PALADIN!!"

"See, was that so hard?"

"PLEASE!! AHAHA, I'M GOING TO DIE-HAHAHA!!"

Lance finally took pity on Keith, but it wasn't entirely altruistic. The blue paladin picked up both of Keith's soles, breaking them out of Stasis, and brought them to his face. The smell of sweat and warmth, with the cinnamon, made his lust take over every rational thought in his head. Lance stuck out his tongue, and began licking away at those twitching, wiggling soles.

"Wahahaha is that?!"

"Mmm! Oh yeah, oh yeah." Lance moaned, trailing his tongue from the bottom of Keith's heel all the way up his sweaty, tender arches, and then licked between all of Keith's toes. "Damn, that is good eatin'."

"Ahaha! Lance! Lance, what a-ahaha-re you doing?!"

"The itching powder is an enzyme, Keith. Gotta denature it, or it'll never go away." Lance popped Keith's toes in his mouth, and suckled them one at a time, indulging in the flavor of Keith's foot sweat and cinnamon. "I don't have any complains if you want to be eternally tickle tortured if you don't."

"Ahaha! Ahaha! W-whatever! Aha! Just get ri-eeheehee-rid of it!"

"Mmh! Oh yeah, they taste fuckin' great, Keith."

Keith kind of wished he was dead. Whether it was the tickling, the itching, Lance's verbal teasing, or the foot-licking, his groin was hot, and he sported a tent like he had never had one before. He couldn't make sense of it, but apparently parts of him kind of liked it. His cock ached, and the front of his red shorts have long since been a sticky mess. His body had betrayed him so much today -- from being held in stasis, to the erection, to the endless spewing of pre. It was still morning; and he was already more exhausted than he was the night before, both mentally and physically.

The only good news for Keith was the itching died down as Lance slurped on his soles. At least Lance wasn't lying about stopping the itching; and the tongue-massage he was being given then was the best thing he had felt in a long time, as much as he hated to admit it. He silently wished that Lance started with this instead, rather than all of the tickling he had to endure for that damn blue paladin's perverted, kinky desires.

And then it dawned on him. The familiar sensation of a spongy, wet material that brushed up and down his feet, and across his toes much earlier.

"..Lance?" Keith spoke up, hiding his face behind his arms. Partly because he couldn't believe what he was about to say.

"Yeah, fearless leader. What?" Lance asked, with Keith's toes still in his mouth, sucking on them as if his life depended on it.

"You licked my feet earlier too, didn't you?"

"…"

"…"

"…"

"Fuckin' foot perv."

Lance braced himself for a surprise attack when he stood in front of Keith's room, ready to return the stolen goods. He was mildly surprised to find Keith sitting on his bed; his hair and face completely messed up, all of which thanks to Lance's games. As soon as Lance unlocked the door and walked in, Keith held out his hands.

"Nuh uh, not so fast!" Lance added, smirking at his team leader.

"What now, Lance?" Keith growled. "Haven't you had enough fun?"

"I want you to agree to a little something first, Keith." Lance started, dangling the bag in which Keith's feet were held. "First of all, from now on, I want you to come over to my room after training, and give *me* a foot rub."

"Foot freak!" Keith accuses, but Lance shrugs it off.

"Second, I want you to let me lick your feet when I ask for them!" Lance continued. "Now that I've had a good taste, I'm addicted. I won't let it go so easily."

"Oh, get fucked, you stupid blue bastard!" Keith threw his wet pillow at Lance, hitting him square in the face.

"Third, if you promise to do that, I will never tickle your feet again. For real. No funny business."

"Again. Get fucked, foot perv!"

"I thought you'd say that." Lance chuckled, and chucked Keith's feet back to their owner. As Keith was busy re-attaching his feet back to the end of his legs, Lance bought out a new toy he had dropped by Pidge to get before coming to see Keith. It looked like a compact mirror that women carried, but instead of a mirror, it emitted a blue glow, and grew brighter when Lance tapped his wrist watch, activating the device.

"What the hell?!" Keith shouted in a raspy voice. The moment

Lance pressed a button, his feet instantly disappeared from his leg again, and re-appeared in Lance's hand, attached to the weird disk.

"Remote recall diskettes." Lance said calmly, to let Keith understand the position he was in. "Either you agree to my terms, or I'll just steal them any time I want, any way, but I also make sure you get a healthy dose of tickling every time. So, tell me, which one would you prefer?"

"... You swear to god you will *never* tickle me again?"

"I will never tickle your yummy, ticklish feet again. I will only give them licks and all of my love. Cross my heart and hope to die. Stick a needle in my eye." Lance brings Keith's foot up to his lips and kisses his toes, lightly, this time, which made Keith's cock hard instantly. "There, sealed with a kiss, and oh, *whoa,* what's this?"

Keith followed Lance's gaze downwards, only to be met with the sight of his shaft standing at full mast once more. His face instantly turns red. The red paladin yanks his foot out of Lance's hand, pops it back on the end of his leg, then grabs the towel laying on the floor to cover himself as he runs towards the bathroom door, slamming it in Lance's face.

"DO WHAT YOU FUCKIN' WANT!"

The End

ABOUT THE AUTHOR

Saber Bhafelheim

Believe it or not, I'm actually a magical black cat with crazy dextrous fingers, here to deliver unto you foot-fuelled fantasies.

www.ingramcontent.com/pod-product-compliance
Lightning Source LLC
LaVergne TN
LVHW020536160826
845677LV00015B/4090

9798848705539